W9-BCS-596

My Feet Are Laughing

Lissette Norman

Pictures by
Frank Morrison

Farrar Straus Giroux
New York

To the loving memory of my mother, Juliana Disla Castillo,
"who lives in heaven now." Her spirit accompanies all my days
—L.N.

To my wife, Connie, and my daughter, Nia
—F.M.

www.fsgkidsbooks.com

Library of Congress Cataloging-in-Publication Data
Norman, Lissette.
    My feet are laughing / Lissette Norman ; pictures by Frank Morrison.— 1st ed.
      p.   cm.
    Summary: Sadie, an imaginative young Dominican American, relates her
experiences growing up in her grandmother's brownstone house in Harlem.
    ISBN-13: 978-0-374-35096-3
    ISBN-10: 0-374-35096-5
    [1. Dominican Americans—Juvenile fiction.   2. Dominican Americans—
Fiction.   3. Grandmothers—Fiction.   4. Harlem (New York, N.Y.)—Fiction.]
I. Morrison, Frank, ill.   II. Title.

PZ7.N78515 Myaf 2006
[E]—dc22

                                                        2004057529

My Name Is Sadie

and I live in Harlem
with my mother
and my little sister, Julie.

Too Much

Aunt Emma—who isn't really my aunt,
but has known my mother for many
   years since before I was born—
said that good girls are seen
and not heard.
I don't think I want to be a good girl,
because I have too much to say.
When the women come over for coffee
and they tell stories and laugh out loud,
I want to talk too,
but I can't join in with grownup folk
because I'm only eight.
But one day they will want to hear all my stories
and they will ask me what I think.
Then the only good girls in our house
will be the girls in the painting on the wall
because I have too much to say.

My Feet Are Laughing

My sister, Julie, is six years old
and copies everything I do.
If I say I like pink dresses,
she says, "I like them too."
My sister, Julie, wants to know why
I can't sit still and my hand is always tapping.
She asked me why I squirm in my seat,
and I said, "Because my feet are laughing."
Julie asks a thousand questions—
it's hard to stop her once she starts.
When I beg her to be quiet,
she says, "Asking questions makes me smart."

Mama Didi's House

Me, Mami, and Julie moved into Grandma's house
because Mama Didi lives in heaven now.
We don't live in a tall apartment building anymore.
Now we live in a big brownstone with high ceilings.
Our steps are inside the house and lead to our own bedrooms.
And we have a small backyard to play in.
I love living in Mama Didi's house—which is our house now.
There are no loud neighbors over our heads,
no more walking up five flights of stairs when the elevator is broken.
And we only moved two blocks away, so I get to see all my friends,
especially my best friend, Crystal.
I love living in Mama Didi's house—which is our house now.
And I don't think I'll ever forget Grandma,
because this house always reminds me of her.

Mami and Pop Are Good Friends

My mother and father are not together anymore,
but they are good friends.
Pop comes over to see me and Julie on weekends
and takes us to the movies or to the zoo.
Mami and Pop told us it would be better if they separated,
and Julie didn't understand it all the way.
She cried for Pop at night until she fell asleep.
At first, I didn't understand it either.
I was really sad about it and was worried
   that I wouldn't see Pop again,
but my parents worked things out and
   I'm not sad anymore.
Even though they are not together,
I know my mom and pop really love us.
I wish we could all live together again,
but Mami said that's not going to happen.
Still, I'm happy that Pop comes to spend time with us
and that Mami and Pop are good friends.

The Things I Love

I love it when Pop calls me silly names
like hoola-hoop head and pumpkin bread
and cock-a-doodle lips and brown sugar dip.
I love it even though that's not my name.
     I love it when I play with Crystal
     and we pretend to be mommies.
     We warm up our baby dolls' bottles
     on my make-believe stove.
     We change their stinky diapers
     and I wipe the baby's nose.
     I love it even though we're not really mommies.
I love it when Mami tries not to wake me up
if I'm napping on the couch.
She whispers on the telephone
and tiptoes through the house.
I love it even though I'm not really sleeping.

Something About My Hair

I love to play with my hair.
My hair has waves and curves and bends
just like a roller coaster ride.
If I twirl my black curls around my finger real fast,
my hair plays some funky music from inside.
But Mami usually straightens it out with a brush.
She puts my hair in two, three, sometimes four ponytails,
depending on how much I fuss.
There's something about my hair that Mami doesn't understand.
And one day, I hid under the bed so she couldn't do my hair.
I was staying there forever; I didn't think that it was fair.
My hair wants to be free of ribbons, I told her,
and wants to do its own thing.
    "If you comb it straight and pull it tight,
      I'm afraid my hair can't sing."
I stayed there for a long, long time,
but eventually Mami had her way.
When I grow up, I'll never brush my hair,
so it can sing its song all day.

Love Is a Lot of Things

Love is Julie crying
for the last piece
of my favorite cherry bubblegum
and me giving it to her.

Love is Crystal telling
Rolando from down the street
that she likes his blue-and-orange jersey
and Rolando wearing it almost every day.

Love is how Mami
takes time to make Pop's
favorite rice pudding
even though they're not together anymore.
That's love!

Bedbugs

Bedbugs
Bedbugs
Julie's scared.
Time to sleep.
She said her prayers,
checked the closet,
and looked under her bed,
but there's no boogie man,
Mami said.
Bedbugs
Bedbugs
They won't bite,
but just in case
she leaves on the light.

The Coolest Job in the World

When I grow up I want to be a poet and write all day long.
　　I will paint pictures with words.
I could write a poem about what makes me happy,
like when Pop takes us to the park.
I can describe anything that I see,
like when a bumblebee kisses a tall sunflower.
　　A poet has the coolest job in the world.
I could write about everything, from the way the sun rises
to how the rain leaves a tiny rainbow in a puddle on my street.
　　In a poem I can say exactly how I feel.
I can write about what is true or I can make stuff up.
I can share some poems and keep some to myself.
Sometimes when I'm sad, I can read a poem and then I feel better.
　　I want to write poems that do that too.
I want to write poems that rhyme and make you want to dance,
and some that don't rhyme, but make you feel like
you can do anything if you only try.
I can write poems about my people who live in Harlem
and my family in the Dominican Republic.
I will recite poems with pretty words that roll right off my tongue.
　　I carry my writing book and pen with me everywhere I go.
I write down all the interesting things I see and hear.
I don't have to wait until I'm older.
　　I can be a poetry girl.
I like being a poet because poets have the coolest job in the world.

Tooth Fairy

Julie is such a scare-dee cat.
She's scared of everything.
Like when her tooth fell out.
Mami told Julie to put it under her pillow
so that the Tooth Fairy can come
and take it while she's sleeping.
She said when Julie wakes up
in the morning, she will find
two shiny quarters that the
Tooth Fairy will leave for her.
But Julie wouldn't go to sleep.
She was up crying and scared
of the Tooth Fairy.
So Mami took Julie's tooth and
Mami put it under her own pillow.
While we slept, the Tooth Fairy
left Julie's quarters under Mami's pillow.
I don't know why Julie is so scared.
I remember I couldn't wait for my teeth
to fall out, so I could get my shiny quarters.
But Julie is such a scare-dee cat.

Giggle Jar

When we lived in our old apartment,
me and Julie shared a room. One night,
Mami told us to stop playing around
and go to sleep. We couldn't laugh out
loud, so we had to giggle. But Mami still
heard us and told us to put all the giggling
away until tomorrow.

     So I thought, *we should put our giggles in a jar.*
     That way we can get them later.
At night, when we're supposed to be sleeping,
I tell Julie silly jokes so she can laugh and
make Mami call out from her room.

     Julie keeps the giggle jar full and
     I guess you can say I do too.
Sometimes, when I'm sad, Julie brings
the giggle jar for me to get some giggles
and I feel better. When Mami's having a
bad day, we give her some giggles too and
she giggles with us.

     But we can have giggles anytime, even
     when we're not sad.

Heaven Is Where Grandma Lives

Heaven is where Grandma lives
where Grandma went to rest.
I'm going to miss my grandma
because Grandma loves me best.
    Heaven better have lots of stores
    with lots of fancy clothes
    because Grandma likes to dress real nice
    and Grandma loves to pose.
No one cooks like Grandma
and if I could visit her, I would.
Her rice and beans and sweet plantains
must have heaven smelling good.
    I thought that Grandma might be sad
    now that she lives so far,
    but Pop said it meant that she was laughing
    when we saw a shooting star.
Grandma's in my heart now.
Pop said it's true.
If that's where Grandma is
then heaven must be there too.
    Heaven is where Grandma lives
    where Grandma went to rest.
    I'm going to miss my grandma
    because Grandma loves me best.

Daydreaming

When I'm in class, I don't always pay attention.
Instead, I stare out the window.
I feel far away and dream I'm a million different things.
I become a twinkling star.
I'm the last cookie in a jar.
I'm a hip-hop song that makes you wiggle.
I'm a late-night sneaky giggle.
I'm a cornrow braid.
I'm a cool glass of sweet lemonade.
I'm a deep and wide ocean.
I'm a magic potion.
I'm a brassy saxophone.
I'm a chocolate-sprinkled ice cream cone.
Then the teacher calls my name and wakes me from my dream.
And I'm just cool with being me.

Dancing Merengue with Mami

Mami works hard all week
so me and Julie wake up early on Saturdays to help her clean the house.
While we clean, Mami plays music and we dance more than we clean.
We listen to fast merengue music and have lots of fun.
Merengue comes from the island of the Dominican Republic
where Mami and Pop were born.
Me and Mami hold hands and Julie dances with the broom.

> *Then we shake our hips from side to side*
> *We shake our hips from side to side*
> > *And turn around and shake side to side*
> > *We turn around and shake side to side*

I love to see Mami laughing when I'm dancing merengue with her
because she's usually serious and tired from working so much.

> *We shake our hips from side to side*
> *And shake our hips from side to side*

Then I switch with Julie and she dances with Mami too.

> *And we shake our hips from side to side*
> *We shake our hips from side to side*
> > *And turn around and shake side to side*
> > *We turn around and shake side to side*

My Name Is Sadie

and I live in Harlem
with my mother
and my little sister, Julie.

E
Norman

Norman, Lissette.

My feet are
laughing.

$16.00

DATE			

12/06

BAKER & TAYLOR